This book belongs to:

....

Note to parents and carers

Read it yourself is a series of classic, traditional tales, written in a simple way to give children a confident and successful start to reading.

Each book is carefully structured to include many high-frequency words that are vital for first reading. The sentences on each page are supported closely by pictures to help with reading, and to offer lively details to talk about.

The books are graded into four levels that progressively introduce wider vocabulary and longer stories as a reader's ability grows.

Ideas for use

- Ask how your child would like to approach reading at this stage. Would he prefer to hear you read the story first, or would he like to read the story to you and see how he gets on?

- Help him to sound out any words he does not know.

- Developing readers can be concentrating so hard on the words that they sometimes don't fully grasp the meaning of what they're reading. Answering the puzzle questions on pages 46 and 47 will help with understanding.

For more information and advice, visit www.ladybird.com/readityourself

Level 3 is ideal for children who are developing reading confidence and stamina, and who are eager to read longer stories with a wider vocabulary.

Special features:

Detailed pictures for added interest and discussion

Hansel and Gretel lived with their father and stepmother in a little house near a wood. Their father was a woodcutter, and he was very poor. They were all very hungry.

Hansel and Gretel went deeper into the wood. They walked for a long time.

In the middle of the wood, they found a house made of sweets and cakes.

Simple story structure

Wider vocabulary, reinforced through repetition

Longer sentences

Educational Consultant: Geraldine Taylor

A catalogue record for this book is available from the British Library

Published by Ladybird Books Ltd
80 Strand, London, WC2R 0RL
A Penguin Company

001 - 10 9 8 7 6 5 4 3 2 1
© LADYBIRD BOOKS LTD MMXI
Ladybird, Read It Yourself and the Ladybird Logo are registered or
unregistered trade marks of Ladybird Books Limited.

ISBN: 978-1-40930-365-7

Printed in China

Hansel and Gretel

Illustrated by Marina Le Ray

Hansel and Gretel lived with
their father and stepmother
in a little house near a wood.
Their father was a woodcutter,
and he was very poor.
They were all very hungry.

One day Hansel and Gretel's father said, "We have no money left. There is no more food for us to eat."

"Then Hansel and Gretel cannot live here," said their stepmother. "We must leave them in the middle of the wood."

"No," said their father.

But their stepmother said, "We must."

Hansel and Gretel were
listening at the door.

"I have a plan," said Hansel,
and he went out to get
some pebbles.

The next day they all went
into the wood.

Hansel dropped pebbles
on the path.

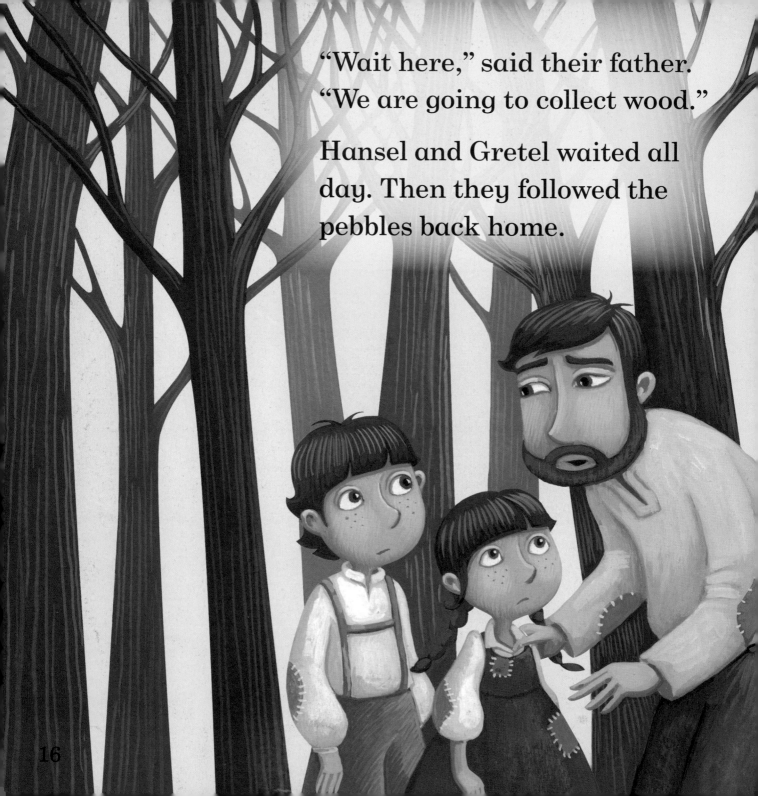

"Wait here," said their father. "We are going to collect wood."

Hansel and Gretel waited all day. Then they followed the pebbles back home.

The woodcutter was glad to see Hansel and Gretel, but their stepmother was angry.

"There is not enough food for us all," she said. "We must take Hansel and Gretel deeper into the wood."

"No!" said their father. "We can't do that."

"We must," said their stepmother. "This time they must not find their way home."

Hansel's stepmother locked the door so that Hansel couldn't get out. He couldn't collect pebbles.

The next day they all went deep into the wood. This time Hansel dropped breadcrumbs on the path.

"Wait here," said their father. "We are going to collect wood."

Hansel and Gretel waited
all day. Then they looked
for the breadcrumbs on
the path.
But the birds had eaten
all the breadcrumbs.

Hansel and Gretel went deeper into the wood. They walked for a long time.

In the middle of the wood, they found a house made of sweets and cakes.

In the house lived a witch. The witch planned to eat Hansel and Gretel.

She locked Hansel in a cage and gave him lots of food.

"Soon he will be fat enough to eat," said the witch. "Then I will cook him in my fire."

"Where is the fire?" said Gretel.

"Here," said the witch.
And she opened the oven door.

"I can't see the fire,"
said Gretel.

The witch opened the
oven door a little wider.

"I still can't see it,"
said Gretel.

The witch opened the oven door as wide as she could.

Gretel pushed her in and locked the door.

Gretel let Hansel out of the cage.

"Look at all this money," said Gretel. "We can take this home and buy food with it."

After a long walk Hansel and Gretel found their way home.

Their father was very glad to see them.

"Your stepmother has gone," he said.

So Hansel and Gretel and their father all lived happily ever after in their little house near the wood.

How much do you remember about the story of Hansel and Gretel? Answer these questions and find out!

- Who did Hansel and Gretel live with at the beginning?

- What did Hansel and Gretel's stepmother want to do with them?

- Can you remember the two different things Hansel dropped on the path?

- What was the witch's house made of?

- How did Gretel get rid of the witch?

Look at the different story sentences and match them to the people who said them.

"Soon he will be fat enough to eat."

"Wait here. We are going to collect wood."

"We must leave them in the middle of the wood."

"I can't see the fire."

"I have a plan."

Read it yourself
with Ladybird

The Three Billy Goats Gruff — Level 1

Cinderella — Level 1

Little Red Hen — Level 1

Goldilocks and the Three Bears — Level 1

The Enormous Turnip — Level 1

The Magic Porridge Pot — Level 1

The Ugly Duckling — Level 1

The Gingerbread Man — Level

Sleeping Beauty — Level

Little Red Riding Hood — Level 2

Sly Fox and Red Hen — Level 2

The Three Little Pigs — Level

Town Mouse and Country Mouse — Level 2

Chicken Licken — Level

The Elves and the Shoemaker — Level 3

Jack and the Beanstalk — Level 3

Hansel and Gretel — Level 3

The Pied Piper of Hamelin — Level 4

The Wizard of Oz — Level 4

Heidi — Level 4

Collect all the titles in the series.